MAMA GOOSE

A NEW MOTHER GOOSE

COLLECTED AND RETOLD BY
Liz Rosenberg

ILLUSTRATED BY
Janet Street

PHILOMEL BOOKS
NEW YORK

For the wonderful Paula Wiseman—L.R.   *For Craig*—J.S.

Philomel Books, Reg. U.S. Pat. & Tm. Off. Published simultaneously in Canada. Printed in Hong Kong by
South China Printing Co. (1988) Ltd.   Text design by Gunta Alexander. The text is set in Berkeley Old Style.
Library of Congress Cataloging-in-Publication Data
Rosenberg, Liz. Mama Goose / collected and told by Liz Rosenberg; illustrated by Janet Street.   p.   cm.   Summary: A collection
of traditional and original nursery rhymes with a feminist slant. 1. Nursery rhymes.   2. Children's poetry.   [1. Nursery rhymes.]
I. Street, Janet, ill.   II. Title. PZ8.3.R726Mam 1994 398.8—dc20 93-11525 CIP AC ISBN 0-399-22348-7
10 9 8 7 6 5 4 3 2 1   First Impression

CONTENTS

Girls and boys come out to play,
The moon is shining bright as day.
Leave your supper, leave your sleep,
And come with your playfellows into the street.
Come with a whoop, come with a call,
Come with a good will or come not at all.
Come let us dance on the open green
And whoever jigs longest shall see what I mean.

Ride away, ride away,
  Jenny shall ride,
She'll have a pussy cat
  Run by her side;
She'll have a little dog
  Trot by the other,
And Jenny shall ride
  To see her grandmother.

Moppety poppet,
Clippity cloppet,
See how my Bobby doth ride!
Up and around and tumble down,
All through the countryside.

Here am I,
Little jumping Joan.
When nobody's with me,
I'm all alone.

Jack and Jill
Went up the hill,
To fetch a pail of water.
Jack fell down,
And broke his crown,
And Jill came tumbling after.

Then up Jill got
And home did trot
As fast as she could caper.
She helped Jack to bed
And mended his head
With vinegar and brown paper.

9

"Where are you going to, my pretty maid?"
"I'm going a-milking, sir," she said.

"May I go with you, my pretty maid?"
"You're kindly welcome, sir," she said.

"What is your father, my pretty maid?"
"My father's a farmer, sir," she said.

"What is your fortune, my pretty maid?"
"My face is my fortune, sir," she said.

"Then I can't marry you, my pretty maid!"
"Nobody asked you, sir," she said.

APPLES 10¢
CRANBERRY PIES 75¢
PLATTERS $1.15

There was an old woman
Lived under a hill,
And if she's not gone
She lives there still.

Apples she sold
And cranberry pies,
And she's the old woman
Who never told lies.

12

Jack Sprat could eat no fat,
His wife could eat no lean.
And so, between the two of them,
They licked the platter clean.

If I had a donkey and he wouldn't go,
Do you think I'd whip him? Oh no, no!
I would feed him oats and hay
And let him stand there all the day.

Baa, baa, black sheep,
  Have you any wool?
Yes sir, yes sir,
  Three bags full;
One for my master,
  And one for my dame,
And one for the little child
  Who lives down the lane.

Off we go on a piggyback ride
Far and fancy free,
Around the world on an empty purse
And back in time for tea.

One,
two,
three,
four, five.
I caught a hare alive.
Six,
seven,
eight,
nine, ten.
I let it go again.
Why did you let it go?
Because it bit my
finger so.
Which finger did
it bite?
The little finger on
the right.

Mary had a little lamb,
Its fleece was white as snow,
And everywhere that Mary went
The lamb was sure to go.

He followed her to school one day
Which was against the rule.
It made the children laugh and play
To see a lamb at school.

And so the teacher turned him out
But still he lingered near,
And waited patiently about
Till Mary did appear.

"What makes the lamb love Mary so?"
The eager children cry.
"Oh, Mary loves the lamb, you know,"
The teacher did reply.

Georgie Porgie, pudding and pie,
Kissed the girls and made them cry;
When Louise came out to play,
Georgie Porgie ran away

There was a little girl,
Who had a little curl
Right in the middle of her forehead;
And when she was good, she was very, very good,
But when she was bad, she was horrid!

There were two blackbirds sitting on a wall,
One named Peter, and the other named Paul;
Fly away, Peter—fly away, Paul.
Come again, Peter—come again, Paul.

Dance to your mommy, Baby,
Dance to your daddy-oh!
You shall have fishy
In a little dishy,
You shall have a fishy
When your boat comes in.
You shall have an apple,
You shall have a plum,
You shall have a rattle
When your folks come home.

Anna Maria, she sat by the fire;
The fire was too hot, she sat on the pot;
The pot was too round, she sat on the ground;
The ground was too flat, she sat on the cat;
The cat ran away with Maria on her back.

Three little monkeys jumping on the bed,
One fell off and bumped his head.
Mama called the doctor
And the doctor said:
"No more monkeys jumping on the bed!"

Three little kittens
They lost their mittens
And they began to cry,
Oh, Mother dear,
We sadly fear
Our mittens we have lost.
What? Lost your mittens?
You naughty kittens!
Well, let's all bake a pie.
Meow, meow, meow!
Never mind, let's have pie.

Rain on the green grass
And rain on the tree,
Rain on the house-top
But not on me.

Hush thee, my baby,
Lie still with thy daddy.
Thy mommy has gone to the mill
To grind thee some wheat
And make thee a treat
So hushabye, baby, lie still.

Diddle diddle dumpling, my son John
Went to bed with his stockings on;
One shoe off and one shoe on,
Diddle diddle dumpling, my son John.

Eat less; breathe more.
Talk less; think more.
Ride less; walk more.
Buy less; wash more.
Worry less; give more.
Preach less; practice more.

Star light, star bright,
First star I see tonight,
Wish I may, wish I might,
Have this wish I wish tonight.

A NOTE TO THE READER

This book was put together by three women who wanted a Mother Goose collection they could read to their own children without wincing.

This meant a goose with her best webbed foot forward, without the wife- and child-beatings, the old people thrown down the stairs, the pecked-at nursemaids (never the kings, you notice). But we wanted to keep the joy of these poems alive, the rhythms and rhymes we knew by heart.

Sometimes it was simply a matter of looking at the old poems in a new way. Other times we lightly edited certain verses, or found wonderful, lesser-known poems to take the place of better-known ones. Mother Goose is a great poet, and can afford to evolve along with the rest of humanity.

These Mother Goose poems have been sorted through and sifted countless times. Ninety percent of the Mother Goose rhymes were current before 1800. We've included two relatively new poems: "No More Monkeys Jumping on the Bed," which has earned its place as a nursery song, and one rhyme of my own (guess which one). The best-known tellers and collectors—Opie, Oxford, Chorao, Greenaway, and so on—chose the selections and versions they liked best. No two editions of Mother Goose are exactly alike. Every generation, every reader changes them a little. But the best survive, keep rising to the top Sort the dross from the gold, and you still find a mine's worth of poetry.

Mother Goose comes from the people and belongs to the people. She is a gentle cousin to the writers of fairy tales and folk tales. Those stories are rooted in danger, violence, punishment, and reward. Not so Mother Goose—a wiser and less predictable inventor. Of course, many of her poems were invented for the nursery, to be chanted and sung to a younger set, as most fairy tales surely weren't. Yet her art is ageless, known and remembered by babies, children, and adults: reinvented every day. Most parents are natural Mother Geese, as are children, teachers, poets. And time, that ruthless anthologizer, ensures that her genius survives.

If poetry is a shining fabric stretched from one end of human time to the other, nursery rhymes are beautiful scraps cut from the whole cloth. They are meant to be sorted through, rearranged, loved, and used—which is what we have done here.

—*Liz Rosenberg*